USING THIS BOOK

*Children learn to read by **reading**, but they need help to begin with.*

When you have read the story on the left-hand pages aloud to the child, go back to the beginning of the book and look at the pictures together.

Encourage children to read the sentences under the pictures. If they don't know a word, give them a chance to 'guess' what it is from the illustrations, before telling them.

There are more suggestions for helping children to learn to read in the *Parent/Teacher* booklet.

British Library Cataloguing in Publication Data

McCullagh, Sheila K.
    The magic penny. — (Puddle Lane. Stage 3; 5)
    1. Readers — 1950-
    I. Title   II. Rowe, Gavin   III. Series
    428.6   PE1119
    ISBN 0-7214-0936-9

First edition

Published by Ladybird Books Ltd Loughborough Leicestershire UK
Ladybird Books Inc Lewiston Maine 04240 USA

© Text and layout SHEILA McCULLAGH MCMLXXXVI
© In publication LADYBIRD BOOKS LTD MCMLXXXVI

The
magic penny

written by SHEILA McCULLAGH
illustrated by GAVIN ROWE

This book belongs to:

Ladybird Books

Jennifer Jane
lived in Puddle Lane.
She lived there with her grandmother.
(Grandmother didn't call her
"Jennifer Jane". She always
called her "Jenny".)

Jennifer Jane
lived in Puddle Lane.
(Grandmother
called her "Jenny".)

One day, Grandmother went out.
"I shan't be home until supper time,
Jenny," said Grandmother.
"Look after the house
until I come back."
She shut the door,
and went off down the lane.

One day, Grandmother went out.

Jennifer Jane began
to tidy up the kitchen.
She cleared the table, and
she washed the dishes.
She polished the chairs, and
she swept up the crumbs.
Then she got a brush,
and began to sweep the fireplace.

Jennifer Jane began
to tidy up the kitchen.

She was sweeping up the ashes,
when something fell down the chimney.
It was small and round,
and covered in black soot.

Something fell down
the chimney.

11

Jennifer Jane picked it up
and looked at it.
"It's a stone from the chimney,"
she said to herself.
She opened the window,
and tossed it out into Puddle Lane.

Jennifer Jane picked it up.
She opened the window, and
tossed it out into Puddle Lane.

13

The rain was raining
in Puddle Lane.
The puddles were full of water.
The little round thing
fell into a puddle.
The water washed off the soot,
and the little round thing
began to shine like silver.

The rain was raining
in Puddle Lane.
The puddles were full of water.

Jennifer Jane
looked out of the window.
She saw the little round thing
shining in the puddle.
"Why, it's a penny!"
cried Jennifer Jane.
"A shining silver penny!"

Jennifer Jane
looked out of the window.
"It's a penny!" she cried.
"It's a silver penny!"

17

Jennifer Jane opened the door, and
went out in the rain,
to look for the silver penny.

Jennifer Jane
went out in the rain
to look for the silver penny.

She found the penny
in less than a minute.
She picked it up.
It shone in her hand like silver.
But as she turned to run back
into the house,
she tripped over a stone,
and fell into a very big puddle!
She sat down right in
the middle of it.

She found the penny
in less than a minute.
She fell in a puddle
and sat down in it.

Poor Jennifer Jane! There she was,
in the middle of a puddle,
and the rain was raining
harder than ever!
But she didn't let go
of the penny.
She held it tightly in her hand.
"I'm very wet," said Jennifer Jane.
"I wish, oh I wish
I was home again!"

"I'm very wet,"
said Jennifer Jane.
"I wish, oh I wish
I was home again!"

Jennifer Jane didn't know it,
but the silver penny was a magic penny.
It had been stolen from the Magician
who lived at the end of the lane.
One of the birds, who lived in the roof
of the old house, had taken it.
But he had dropped it just
as he was flying over the chimney
of Jennifer Jane's house.
As soon as Jennifer Jane said,
"I wish I was home again,"
she found herself flying through the air.

The silver penny
was a magic penny.

In less than a minute, Jennifer Jane
found herself safely home again,
by the fireplace in the kitchen.

In less than a minute,
Jennifer Jane
found herself safely
home again.

She was still very wet,
but she didn't cry.
She lit the fire, and then
she sat down beside it,
until she was quite dry.

She was very wet,
but she didn't cry.
She sat by the fire
until she was dry.

Jennifer Jane looked out
of the window.
It was still raining hard
in Puddle Lane.
"I won't go out in the rain again,"
she said. "Poor Grandmother!
She'll be **very** wet."

"I won't go out
in the rain again,"
said Jennifer Jane.

Jennifer Jane picked up the magic penny.
(She had put it down on the table.)
"I wish dinner was ready," she said.
"I wish it was on the table.
And I do wish Grandmother was home."
In less than a minute,
there was the dinner
ready on the table!

Jennifer Jane said,
"I wish dinner was on the table."
And in less than a minute,
dinner was on the table.

Just at that moment,
Grandmother opened the door.
"What **have** you been doing, Jenny?"
she cried. "And where did you get
that dinner?"

Grandmother opened the door.

So Jennifer Jane told her grandmother
all about the magic silver penny.
"Put it away carefully, Jenny,"
said Grandmother.
"We may have to use it again."
So Jennifer Jane put the silver penny
in the little china shoe
that stood on the mantelpiece.
She **did** use it again –
but that is another story.

Jennifer Jane
put the silver penny away.

When the Magician who lived in the
old house at the end of Puddle Lane
heard the story of Jennifer Jane,
he laughed to himself.
"So that's where my magic penny went,"
he said.

the Magician

The Magician made up a rhyme
about what happened to Jennifer Jane.
He wrote it down in his book.

This is the rhyme:
Jennifer Jane
lived in Puddle Lane.
(Grandmother
called her "Jenny".)

Jennifer Jane
went out in the rain
to look for a silver penny.

She found the penny
in less than a minute.
She fell in a puddle
and sat down in it.

"I'm very wet,"
said Jennifer Jane.
"I wish, oh I wish
I was home again!"

In less than a minute,
Jennifer Jane
found herself safely
home again.

She was very wet,
but she didn't cry.
She sat by the fire
until she was dry.

"But I won't go out
in the rain again,"
said Jennifer Jane.

Notes for the parent/teacher

Turn back to the beginning, and print the child's name in the space on the title page, using ordinary, not capital letters.

Now go through the book again. Look at each picture and talk about it. Point to the caption below, and read it aloud yourself.

Run your finger along under the words as you read, so that the child learns that reading goes from left to right.

Encourage the child to read the words under the illustrations. Don't rush in with the word before he/she has had time to think, but don't leave him/her struggling.

Read this story as often as the child likes hearing it. The more opportunities he/she has of looking at the illustrations and **reading** the captions with you, the more he/she will come to recognise the words.

If you have several books, let the child choose which story he/she would like.

"No, "I live in the Map at the end of Puddle Lane. But I always come here on Fridays. They have cheese and nuts in the market on Fridays. Come and see."

Jeremy looked down. He looked at one of the tables. There was a big cheese at one end of the table, and a basket of nuts at the other end.

Jeremy looked down.

17